Jeremy Meets Abigail

John Gumbs

Published by John Gumbs
Publishing partner: Paragon Publishing, Rothersthorpe
First published 2023

ISBN 978-1-78792-010-1

Book design, layout and production management by Into Print
www.intoprint.net
+44 (0)1604 832149

Contents

For Heidi who set me on the road writing

Chapter 1

Jeremy Meets Abigail

THIS WAS THE weekend Jeremy knew he had the chance of meeting a lovely girl, and making something out of it. He had been going out with his friends every weekend, and had failed to meet the girl of his choice. All the others had already met the girls that they wanted to meet. Only he alone now was left to try to see what he can do. He looked in the mirror and was pleased that he was dressed okay. He said to himself, *it has to be this weekend. Can't leave it any longer.*

Leaving his flat, he met up with the other boys just outside the disco. They chatted and joked for a while, then they entered the place. It was packed with many boys and girls.

Jeremy looked around and saw that most were regulars that he saw every weekend. But there was one, she was new, and he kept his eyes upon her. No one knew her, so they couldn't give any information about her. Jeremy approached her as soon as she got to the bar, and sat on a stool that was vacant.

"I haven't seen you here before," Jeremy said to her.

"This is my first time here," she turned to him and said, "and *you* are?"

"Oh! I am Jeremy. Nice to meet you!"

She told him that her name was Abigail.

"That is such a nice name," he told her.

"Are you from around these parts or from another place?" Jeremy asked. "Most the boys and girls comes from the outlying places."

"I got my own car. I'm from the village not far away from here. Would you like a dance?"

"Yes, please." Jeremy didn't hesitate. As he took Abigail and went over to where the others were dancing, he noticed that they were all pleased that he had found a girl.

At the end of the disco they always end up at somebody's flat. This weekend, it was Jeremy's flat. There were about three other couples and a few singles. Inside the flat everyone started looking at the collection of music Jeremy had. He was a real lover of music. There was nothing missing in his collection. CD after CD went on and everyone was busy with their own way of dancing. When not dancing, the conversation moved from one subject to the next. They had already agreed not to talk about religion when they were together at the weekends, it was too confusing a subject, and it spoiled the fun.

*

Saturday morning around 3 am, Jeremy and Abigail were left alone. "I'll make some coffee," he said to her.

"I'll have some tea."

After a while he came back with the coffee and tea. He set them on the coffee table and sat down next to Abigail. "Did you enjoy the evening?" he asked her.

"Yes, I like it very much. Do you do this often?"

"Every weekend," Jeremy told her. "We take turns at each other's place."

"Have you ever had a girlfriend?" Abigail asked.

Jeremy said, "No. I'm just starting out. What about you?"

"My first boyfriend lasted two months. He was becoming too serious at a time when I was deep in my studies. To me, my studies were more important than a relationship. That could come later."

"True! Depending on what sort of relationship it is. I believe just like you, that study is more important. Get it over and done with."

Abigail said, "So you're young and untouched, that's interesting!"

"Why?"

"Because you've never been with a woman," Abigail told him plainly.

"Is that good or bad?" he asked her.

"Haven't you heard about it? Did no one ever talked to you about it? My mother taught me a lot."

"It's only since I met the others that we talked a lot about many things."

"Don't worry," Abigail told him. "Later, when you meet the right woman, then you'll understand."

Jeremy knew that Abigail was a nice girl. She had eyes that were grey, and her brown hair came down at both sides of her face. To him she looked like one of those pretty models you see in the magazine. He like her, and she sensed it too, but she was waiting to see what he would do. Jeremy didn't want to make a fool of himself and rush in, to find a 'NO' sign. He decided to play the waiting game, take it easy.

Abigail, a smart young girl, knew how to go along with boys.

"What will she do?" Jeremy asked.

Abigail smiled, "That's when all the heavens break loose, and you're about to find yourself in bloody pain."

"She's going to attack me, you mean?"

"Not that sort of attack. This one is between boy and girl. This is one of those days when you're going to lose it," she told him. "You're going to have your first encounter with a girl."

"Oh, *my!*" he said, as he poured another cup of coffee for Abigail. "You joining us again tonight?" he asked her.

"Yes, I'll be there. I have to drive home first.

Chapter 2

The Weekend Hike

SATURDAY NIGHT THEY all met at the disco. Abigail was there too. She hugged Jeremy, took him up to the bar, and bought him a drink. Later, they were dancing, and spinning around on the dance floor.

Abigail said, "You dance pretty well. I like it!"

Jeremy was so pleased to hear that coming from Abigail. "You are not a bad dancer yourself," he told her. A few minutes later, they went for a stroll and back. All the others were now happy for Jeremy. He was getting on well with Abigail.

At the flat of Carl, they gathered and the party carried on. Jeremy learned that Abigail likes hiking and walking a lot.She likes to be out in the wild enjoying nature with not too many people around. Jeremy had never done that sort of thing, but if Abigail can do it, why can't he? All the others heard about it and thought it was a good idea to go away for the weekend hiking. They all got the clothes and equipment they needed. On the map, they picked an area, and how far it would be to walk. They planned to start on the Friday afternoon, and stay out till Sunday evening. The area that they picked was a good one. It wasn't far from a main town, but still far enough to be on your own. Some walks were across low mountains with beautiful views.

*

The following weekend they all set out, 13 of them, to spend their time in the wild. Everyone had their own tent and kit. All the gear that they needed. They came across a stream with many strewn rocks. From one rock to the other they stepped across. Jeremy slipped and his foot went into the water awkwardly, and was jammed between other rocks. Carefully, the others helped, and they managed to cross over without any more hindrance.

Arriving at the place they had picked, they set up camp. It wasn't long before they had a fire going and everyone was there around it. They planned to set out very early in the morning on a long trek. Everyone had their own mobile to keep in touch with home, and with each other.

Early Saturday morning everyone was up, and they were off on a long hike. Now and again they would rest and chat about anything, except the one subject they all avoided at weekends.

With the back pack on leaning on a tree, Abigail waited while Jeremy caught up with her. She said to him, "Do you find it hard? Not many more kilometres to go."

"It is hard, yes, but I'm enjoying it."

"Good," she said, and touched him on the shoulder.

They came down a small mountain track, and then up on the other side. There was a small drop just to the right, and as Abigail came along, it gave way, and she tumbled over trying to get hold of anything that would help break her fall. She screamed as she went down. Landing on ground that wasn't safe, there was another big drop below her. It was possible she could fall over this drop if she didn't control herself, and moved too furiously. All the others came around, and was now sorting out a plan how to get Abigail out from where she was. They called out to her, *"Are you okay?"*

"So far, yes, I'm okay. Nothing damage as far as I know." It wasn't easy trying to get down to where she was, but they managed somehow with some ropes to pull her back out. It wasn't long before she was back with the others, with no real damage done to her, laughing and joking. They reminded her that she was lucky, for had the drop been deeper, it would have been more difficult to try to rescue her. They would have had to get the rescue team out.

Jeremy hugged Abigail, and kissed her on her cheek. "Glad you're okay!," he said. "Luck was on your side!"

"Thanks, " she replied. "I thought that was it."

*

The next weekend the group gathered together, Abigail wasn't there. Jeremy wondered where she could be. Had anything happened to her? All the others were also worried. Two weeks later, she turned up and told Jeremy that she was having some problem with her old boyfriend. He just wouldn't leave her alone and let her get on with her life.

"I tried to get you on the mobile without any luck," Jeremy told her. "Do you want me sort that boyfriend out for you?"

Abigail smiled. They were sitting outside on the benches.

"That's real nice of you, but this is something I have to sort out for myself. And remember, you are only just starting out in life, and have a lot to learn."

"With you, I could learn a lot. I'll let you teach me!"

"What can I teach you except … Oh! … No! … *That?* … It could be a disaster!"

"Do you think I'm that bad?"

"How would I know that, Jeremy? We haven't even kiss, so I wouldn't really know."

"Would you be angry if I kiss you now?"

"You should ask me, 'can I kiss you?' Then I would think about it, and say yes or no."

"Can I kiss you, Abigail?"

"Yes, you can, Jeremy."

Jeremy's heart was now beating faster. He never thought he would have gotten the chance to kiss Abigail. The chance was there sometime later, if they got on well, to kiss, and to take it to the next stage. But now he was overwhelmed.Jeremy leaned slightly to his left, touched Abigail lightly, kissed her lower lips, then her upper, she gave him her tongue, he gave her his, and it became passionate.

"WOW!" she exclaimed. "I never knew you had it in you. That was out of this world. For someone who has never been with a woman, you really know how to kiss."

"So, I've passed. I can be your boyfriend now?"

"Jeremy, yes, you can. Oh! There's one thing – no sex before marriage!"

"You're not serious?" Jeremy said. "Not even a teeny bit?"

"No. Nothing. You'll just have to wait, that is my rule," she said.

"And what if we don't get that far?"

"Hard luck for you then, but I do hope we get there. I'm beginning to like you."

"That's a good start," Jeremy said. "Suppose we should court for more than a year?"

"The rule still stand," she told him.

Abigail wasn't like the other girls. She was strict when it came to whom you go to bed with. She was interested in a family, and the man, who she happens to join up with should know straight out, that he could not jump into bed with her whenever he felt like it.

"We'll be sleeping together, won't we? I mean when we get married."

"Ah! There you go," Abigail said, "talking about hitching up. I have only said, I'm beginning to like you."

"I like you very much," Jeremy told her.

"Thanks for telling me.'

It was time for them to depart with the others to someone's flat. They all left and went to Irene's flat. The flat wasn't that big, but had enough room to house 13 people. They squatted here and there, and started conversation about groups and bands. Later, they talked about the hiking experience and what had happened to Abigail. Listening to the different music, they started planning to go to some big city, they picked London, so now they all agreed that that is what they will do.

Chapter 3

The Group Goes To London

LONDON IS A massive city. Jeremy and Abigail – in fact all the others – had never been there in person before. They had all heard of it, but had never ever been there. The train left the station where they all boarded late in the afternoon. It took about two hours and five minutes to get to St. Pancras in London.

Taking an underground train, they headed for the Embankment. Hearing music as they came out of the station, they went to investigate. There was a band playing in the gardens next to the station.

Looking across the water, they saw the London Eye slowly moving. The group then went up the road towards the Big Ben. Excited, they chatted along the way pointing out unusual sights. At the top of the road, they saw to their left, Boudica, the warrior queen who fought against the Romans. Many of the group had heard and read the story. On their right, slightly left, were the buildings of Parliament. The statue of Churchill they saw, and commented on it.

This group like walking, and they knew they had many kilometres to walk, and seeing the sights. They looked around, taking in all that they could see.

Westminter Abbey was right there, staring back at them,

the Cenotaph, the resident of the Prime Minister wasn't far away.Then they went up to Trafalgar Square.

Sitting around on the fountain, they really liked London. Just on the left was the National Museum. Many of them were into art, and many hours would be spent looking around. Slightly to the east was St. Martin-in-the-Fields church; South African House; and the Canada House.The South West was the Mall leading to Buckingham Palace. Charing Cross Road went between the National Gallery and the church. The group stared a long time at Nelson's column. The square was named from the battle which took place in 1805. The group were enjoying every minute of what they saw, and they now realized that all of London could not be seen in one day. On their way up to the High street, they found a pub with tables outside, so they gathered themselves there, and ordered what they wanted.

After leaving the pub, they came upon the High Street, and went immediately into one of the big music places. They had never seen anything as big as that.Organizing themselves, they decided not to spend a long time looking around. From one side of the street to the next, they walked. There was a disco place, it was massive, they liked it. This was where they would spend the night, and cool off, after they had walked around. They had found themselves a nice place to stay and was happy with it. Now they had seen for themselves how big London was. They could not see everything all at once, that was not possible.

At the disco the music was very loud, but that didn't bother them, they were accustomed to that. Abigail said to Jeremy while they were seated, "It's a big place, isn't it? I mean London. I am pleased with what I have seen."

"There's quite a lot more to come according to the guide book. We might have to come back another time in order to see more of it."

"Are you enjoying yourself?" she asked him.

"Yes, with you, and the rest of this group, it is fantastic."

"Glad to hear!" She had to raise her voice a bit.

After spending some time in the disco, they all came out, found that Jamie was missing. It was strange because he had entered the disco with them. Jamie was one of the singles, he had no girlfriend. He had a lovely nice face, always smiling, with black curly hair.

Out on the High Street there were many people going to and fro, making it hard to get through the crowd. Back in the disco, the group asked around, but no one knew anything about Jamie's whereabouts. They had seen him, that's all. Every member in the group knew that they had to report whenever they intended going off on their own. That was the rule. All must stay together, and inform each other if they were going away.

The group got word that someone had seen Jamie talking to a red head girl before they left. They had taken the side door. At least the group know he was alive and okay. But he need to make contact with them. Why didn't he use his mobile? The group walked on until they came to the end of the High Street on the corner of Marble Arch.

The road on their right led up to Edgware station. They stood outside a cinema. Leaning on the railings that barred the people from the traffic, an open car with a red head driving with Jamie beside her, turned into the street leading up to Edgware station. Jamie saw the group through the crowd, started waving, and calling out, and later, the car pulled in a few metres up.

Crossing the road with its heavy traffic, for there were many buses behind each other along with trucks and other such vehicles. All pleased to see Jamie, hugs were many. Carl told him off for not letting the group know what was taking place. Jamie introduced the red head as his new girlfriend. She had a flat down in Paddington and the group were invited to come there that evening. Jamie gave them the address, and the car drove away. Carl said, "That girl is strange, but seems to be rich, hope Jamie knows what he's doing!"

It was around 6:30 pm when the group found themselves on the Essex road, and in front of the address they had been given. Carl went up and push the door bell. He hadn't seen the car at the side.

It was on the other side in a residents' park. The door opened and the red head, Charlotte, was there with a pretty smile. Jamie was there beside her. "Come on in" Charlotte said. "Plenty of room here!"

"Thanks!" Carl said, as he made his way in, followed by the rest. The house was four storeys high. Charlotte lived on the bottom floor while the other floors were taken up for rent. The top floor was vacant with plenty of space. Charlotte explained to them how she came by the house and was glad she bumped into Jamie. Carl let her know what the group did when they were back home.

Charlotte found it exciting and was given the go ahead to visit them. Of course, this was all because of Jamie. Everyone liked the place where Charlotte lived. It wasn't very far from the main railway station, and there were many discos around.

After chatting for about an hour, they all went out and found a nice disco. Charlotte got well in with the group, like how they organize themselves, and was very pleased.

There was a big music festival in Hyde Park, and the group went to it. Having enjoyed the festival it was time to depart from London. They all promised that they'll return for they had enjoyed themselves, and there was much more still to be seen. Jamie had invited Charlotte down whenever she had free time, she accepted the offer.

Chapter 4

Jeremy And Abigail Tie The Knot

BACK AT THEIR own place, the group settled down and again went on long hikes. It was disco night and they all were there. After the disco had ended, they all ended up at Jamie's flat. It was just big enough to house the group. No one complained as they began to talk, listen to music, making comments, and just enjoying the night.

The next week on the Wednesday they all met to watch an International Cricket match. Then they began to talk about the fair that was held in October in Kingston-Upon-Hull. Everyone was willing to go.

*

It was Europe's largest travelling fair, lasts for one week. The group were all on time to catch the train. The journey was about three hours and some minutes. Arriving at Kingston-Upon-Hull, and getting to where the fair was, they were surprised how big it was. The goose fair at their place was very big – but this one at Hull was even bigger.

Warned by Carl not to stay too far from each other, to let each other know where they were, they set off looking at all the attractions. From one turnstile to the next, they all took turn. Not every one went on the big dipper, too scary for some. Just before they left an announcement was made: *Jeremy and Abigail were going to get married.*

Before the marriage of Jeremy and Abigail took place, Jamie brought Charlotte down, and the group went on a hike. After the hike, it was disco time, then to a flat.

A month later, the wedding of Jeremy and Abigail took place. Every member of the group was there, and it turned out to be a good day. On the night of the wedding when both Jeremy and Abigail were alone, Abigail said to Jeremy, "Now it's all yours, you've waited a long time."

Jeremy smiled, "Yes it was a long time." He picked Abigail up in his arms, and carried her to the bedroom. He laid her on the bed, and went next beside her. She turned and looked at him, "Aren't you going to do anything?"

Jeremy said, "What can I do? I don't know where to start!"

Abigail said, "You know how to kiss, and that wasn't bad at all. Now you have permission to do more."

He smiled at her. "You were really strict of not going to bed before marriage, and now you're giving it all away!"

"To my husband, and no one else. Get cracking or I shall fall asleep."

Jeremy took Abigail, wrapped her up in his arms and started kissing her. Abigail love this, she love the way Jeremy kiss. But she realized he was very slow in moving on. Something she was really longing for, and her husband was a bit slow in performing his marital duties.

Abigail said, after they had kissed, "So I'll be the first woman you've ever been with. Nothing to worry about, just take your time."

Abigail was shocked, surprised when she saw what her husband had. She could have burst out laughing, but she didn't do so. She said softly to him, "This is the start of making our first baby."

Jeremy wasn't ashamed anymore. He trusted Abigail, his wife, and she guided him along. As the days went by, Jeremy learned a lot.

Jeremy and Abigail broke the news to the rest of the group letting them know that Abigail was pregnant. They started dancing around and patting Jeremy. Some even were speculating that it could be twins. Around this time, four members came up with the idea of forming a music group.

Chapter 5

The Music Group

THESE FOUR MEMBERS were very good with music, and the other members didn't object to the idea of them having a music group. They thought it was a good thing to do. It wasn't hard to find an empty place to practise. There were many halls around. The nearest one to the group wasn't that far away. Having bought the instruments they set up, and began practising on a Friday night. For months and months they practise and became very good. All the other members of the group were amazed how these four boys excelled themselves in the music. Their first gig was at a youth club and it was a hit. Everyone there were pleased. The music group now had a repertoire, and played in many places.

At one of their hiking trips, on the last night, the group were all in a circle around a burning fire. Two of the music group had brought their acoustic guitars with them. They started playing, and they all started singing.

Everyone knew after they had returned that the band was heading for the big time. The music group was still hoping to get themselves a recording contract. Carl took over as manager, and the music group agreed that they'll stay with the others no matter what takes place. Bookings were now coming in from all over. There was one from Hamburg in Germany.

Carl said to the group, "You all are going to really enjoy this trip. It is fabulous. Something that you'll always remember. And for our musicians, they'll love it. Opportunities galore. At the festival there are many events going, you shall never be bored."

Jeremy said, "Sounds fantastic, can't wait to get there!"

Carl said, "There are many ways for us to travel, but I think the quickest is to get on a flight."

*

In Germany, Carl checked that everyone was present. After accomodations, they all went round to check. The Reeperbahn festival was one of Europe's biggest festival, held in September, with over 900 events They found out where and when the music group had to play. Everyone began liking the place, it was really cool, and exciting. The band performed well at three different places.

Everyone liked them, and they ended up with a record contract.

Back at home, Jeremy and Abigail were preparing for their first child. The music group's first recording was creeping up in the top 10 charts at number 5. They all decided that the trip to Hamburg was well worth it. And that it was breathtaking and enjoyable. Not long after the recording contract Abigail brought forth a son, and gave it the name Thomas. The whole group celebrated.

Thomas was a half year old when the whole group went out to hike. Abigail stayed in camp along with a couple other girls. The route the group took was beautiful, plenty of greenery and small mountains. Everyone found it a very enjoyable hike. It was hard, but they all made it.

Two weeks later, the hiking group was out again, this time Abigail took part. They had to cross a river that was not very long, but dangerous to cross. The ropes had been tied securely, and the river below was fast flowing. Jeremy and the others were already across. Abigail got onto the rope, and started moving across. Halfway over the river she panicked, she said that she couldn't hold on any longer. Jeremy and the others were coaching her. She had crossed rivers many times before without any problems, but for some unknown reason, this one was giving her trouble.

"Hold on, don't let go," was the command to her.

"I can't," she said. "I'm going to let go."

Jeremy was already making plans to go and assist her, but it was too late. Abigail let go of her hold on the rope, and plunged down into the fast flowing river.

Jeremy immediately went in, but was pulled away from her into the bank he had just come from. Abigail struggled, she was a good swimmer, and she was lucky that she didn't go down to the next level where all the rocks were. She was swept furiously into the far bank still with the backpack strapped on. She stayed there, and was glad that she was safe, now out of harm's way. Jeremy too, was okay. The group managed to get themselves back in one piece, and was on their way. Abigail ended up with a few bruises, but she wasn't seriously hurt.

*

Charlotte was down again from London, and Jamie was over the moon. The group went out discoing and, as usual, ended up at one of the member's flat. The music group was really catching on. They had a contract to play in Brussels, Amsterdam and Paris. Not all the members of the group were available to go this time. Abigail found it okay for Jeremy to go, so did Charlotte, letting Jamie go along.

*

Carl had everything arranged, and the group arrived in Brussels, and went down well. In Amsterdam, they were a big hit, picked up many fans. The last venue in Paris was absolutely amazing. Then they returned home.

The music group was now popular at home, and began to become the same in Europe. Arrangements were being made for a tour of America, in New York. But before that, the whole group were planning a hike. They all loved hiking, the outdoors, fresh air, healthy, good for the mind and body.

There were discussions about the bands and groups that were around in the 60s. Charlotte was young, but she heard from her parents about certain groups that had made the big time. In fact, she had some of their records. The Beatles of course were famous, so was Pink Floyd, and the Rolling Stones. The music group knew that they had a different sound, and that attracted the young ones more than anything else. Many more famous groups were around as well, including singers.

*

The whole group went out well-equipped for the hike.

Setting up camp at a certain place, they left a few to look after it. Aiming for a 30 kilometre hike, the group set off, and after three kilometres, they came to their first river crossing. This one had to be walked across. It was flowing down normal, so there was no problem in crossing over. Inside every backpack were the things that were necessary in case of emergency. Many changes of socks, first aid kit, water bottle, and lots of other important things.

The first couple of kilometres saw the group on level ground as they walked along. Then they rose higher up, and took the path that led to the top of a high mountain. Halfway through the hike there was something wrong with Charlotte, but later on, she recovered, and the hike carried on.

From the top of the mountain they went down to lower ground, crossed a stream, then into some thick woods for about three kilometres. At the end of the hike, everyone was accounted for. They walked back to their camp feeling fit in mind and body.

Back at home the group went to a disco, and ended up at one of the member's flat. There they talked about music, the last hike, the coming tour and other important things.

It was now time for the music group to be off on their American tour which would last about two months. Their girlfriends would accompany them along with others from the group. The Americans always treated foreign groups in a good way, and this group enjoyed how they were taken care of. They played in a great big stadium where the fans went wild. After playing in a few more places, and the tour was up, they all returned home.

Mountain Surge was the name of the music group's band. They had just come back from an American tour. They were doing great in the charts in their country, and in Europe.

Chapter 6

The Fifty Kilometres Hike

THE WEDDING OF Charlotte and Jamie took place six months after they came back from America. Just like all the weddings it went down well, and there was much entertaining. After the wedding, and the music group had nothing on their agenda, they all arranged a 50 kilometres hike. Preparations began. Carl warned everyone to make sure that they were in a fit state. They had to do some side training as well. Plenty of water must be taken, good socks and boots.

"The hike will be done in stages, for it will get really hard. Camp will be set up as usual."

*

No one could have asked for such beautiful weather that the group had on the first stage of the hike. It was cool and lovely. They were all fit, in a good mood, and ready to go. For Abigail, this hike was important. She wanted to finish it without any mishap. She was in good shape, and ready to take it on. Charlotte too, had done well in the hikes that they had undertaken. Now, after her marriage, she was attempting this 50 kilometre hike. It was going to take place in stages, and she was glad for that. Camp will be set up at the end of every stage. Everyone will be checked to see if they are okay.

Walking is good, it makes you feel good; sets you in a good mood. That is a fact, and the whole group knew it to be so. Early in the morning around 5.30 am the group set out for the first stage.

They were all very enthusiastic chatting away merrily for the first walk. It all went well. No one dropped out. Only a bit tired. Carl was very pleased with their performance, and he told them so.

The group themselves were also amazed that they managed to complete the first stage without any problems. Blisters were checked and dealt with. And the group prepared themselves for the following day. They had planned to eat up those kilometres in three days. With the first 15 kilometres behind them, they were now looking forward to attack the rest.

They knocked off the next 15 kilometres with no problems whatsoever, and were very pleased with themselves. Now they only had 20 kilometres left, and they knew that that was going to be a tough one. On that day when they started out on the 20 kilometres, everyone fit and able, with no complications at all. Halfway through, Charlotte had a cramp, and had to relax for a while. Charlotte's lower leg did give her much pain. It was massaged, and ice was put on it. Eventually, the pain left the leg, and she was able to walk as before.

The group's aim now was to finish off the rest of the kilometres. The weather had turned a bit cloudy, but it stayed dry. After a couple of tests, Charlotte was now confident in finishing the rest of the walk. On the last five kilometres,

Charlotte's foot played up again. This time, she took it very slow, and finished the walk. At the camp, everyone congratulated her, as they prepared to enjoy the evening, like they always do. Abigail was super fit, and mastered the 50 kilometres. Jeremy promised her something special when they get back.

In the evening, they were all together with a small lake where they chatted over the 50km walk; played and sang songs, down until early morning the next day.

The next weekend saw them all at one of the member's place. They did what they normally do chatting, listening to music, commenting, and most of all about the coming gigs for the music group. Then they will go the local pub and discos and enjoy themselves. Soon, the music group will be off to the Midlands for another gig.

In the East Midlands the music group played at Nottingham and Leicester.

Chapter 7

The Killer Walk

WHILE THE MUSIC group was still in the Midlands, Carl was over in the Netherlands. He had arranged for the whole group to be in Nijmegen. The four days marches were soon to take place. Arriving back on the Friday, he met the group at their usual place. He gave them all the information. This was going to be the killer walk for the group. They would have to walk 50 kilometres per day for four days.

Some of the group weren't pleased to hear that news because they had not so long ago struggled to walk 50 kilometres, and that was done in stages. What about Abigail and the rest? Would she be able to tackle it? Carl told them that they could do it. All they need was some good training, and he warned them to start doing it now.

The group was tough and they had never ever backed out of taking part in such a challenge. Abigail and Charlotte knew that it wasn't going to be easy, but their spirits were high.

Carl gave more information: the music group will play. Everyone will enjoy the trip. The people are very friendly, and it's the oldest place in the country.

The following week the group began their training. It was

hard, but they coped with it. Around this time the music group had become very rich, and was recording a new album. Weeks upon weeks of training the group were now super fit.

They were now ready for the Nijmegen walk.

Schiphol was only an hour's flight away and the group arrived there without any problems. They were driven from Schiphol down to Nijmegen and to the place where they would stay.

The month is July. The group was up very early the first day to start out on their walk. Completing the first 10 kilometres was tough. It was very interesting to see so many walkers. Charlotte and Abigail were doing fine so far. Jamie was struggling. A few others found it hard. At the end of the 50km, all in the group made it, shattered and hurting. The sun had already set, and there were still many walkers hopping along.

In the evening of that first day, a check was made to see that no one had blisters, and that their feet were okay. Abigail said that she was surprised to see so many older people walking.

On the second day early, the group was up and were on a new route. The route was packed with people, old and young. This inspired the whole group to do their best. This second day of walking was a real test for the group. Every single one of them had to dig in to complete the route. That evening, the music group played, and it was enjoyable. The morning of the third day was a bit hot. They made sure that they had enough water, and that they should get into a good steady walk.

This third day's walk became hard for the group. They were in aches and pain, but managed to finish it. There they all were, moaning and groaning. Three days had taken a lot out of them, the fourth day was still waiting to be tackled.

Friday, the last day of the walk was a fairly good day. Although there were many clouds in the sky, there was no rainfall. This was the day – make or break. The group had done something they had never done before. Walking three days at 50km per day was really something. Now the last day would make it four days, and they all wanted very much to finish it.

The roads were jampacked with walkers. Many struggling on this last day. Inside the city, people had already taken their seats to watch as the walkers finish. Family and friends gave out flowers. The TV cameras were there as well. Along the way, the group was doing well until about 10 kilometres to go, Abigail had to pull up. Her right foot went funny. She felt as though she had torn something. A couple of the group stayed back with her, while the others went further. medics came and advised her to end the walk. But Abigail insisted that she could finish the course. She was taking a big chance. This was now leading to pushing the body too far. The muscles would be now feeling like putty. Rest is the main ingredient.

The medics gave their good advice, but Abigail started hopping along. She managed to knock another kilometre off. The pain was now becoming unbearable – you could see it in her face – she showed it.

Everyone knew Abigail, she was a tough one. The four days' marches have proven to be a tough call. Stubbornly, with an injured leg, she would not give in. Holding fast to

Jeremy around the shoulders, and with him holding her fast around the waist, she hopped along.

Both sides of the road was lined with spectators. People calling out, wishing 'good luck!'

There were now six kilometres left. This was a day that Abigail would never ever forget in her life. Still struggling, very slowly, she managed a few more kilometres.

At last, with one kilometre to go, the pain became terrible. Abigail held on, and managed somehow to give a smile as she eased her way to the finish line. She was surrounded by people whom she didn't know, giving her flowers and congratulating her. The rest of her group was there too. Clive was awfully pleased that all the members in the group made it to the end. They'll remember this four days' marches, all of their lives.

There were still the blisters dance, and the whole evening of this Friday to enjoy. All the attractions and music, it is something that one should experience. It is just amazing.

Watching the many people trying to dance on their blisters was a real laugh. But that is what it was all for. Even Abigail went over, and hopped a few times. Charlotte had sympathy for Abigail. She was glad that Abigail made it to the end. It was Abigail's fighting spirit that got her there. Jamie had a couple of blisters. They did not prevent him from finishing. All the other members in the group were well, and pleased with themselves.

After the festival had ended, Clive had everything arranged. The group was to travel from Schiphol to Heathrow. Seeing that Charlotte and Jamie lived in London, they stayed there, then went back to their own place. And of course, when

Jeremy and Abigail got back they were glad to see their son Thomas.

The group met again as usual, with the music group very, very famous. They did not give up their walking. More weddings took place within the group.

Also by John Gumbs

Side By Side 978-1-78222-845-5
Jehanne 978-1-78222-571-3
The Trial and Burning of Jehanne 978-1-78222-609-3
Aitch H 978-1-78222-628-4
Jay G 978-1-78222-656-7
Heidi 978-1-78222-682-6
Sheila 978-1-78222-729-8
Just Mates 978-1-78222-751-9
Jay G, Assignment to the Netherlands 978-1-78222-782-3

Past
Future
SIDE BY SIDE
Short stories and Poems
JOHN GUMBS

JEHANNE
John Gumbs

THE TRIAL AND BURNING OF
JEHANNE
John Gumbs

AITCH

Jay
G
John Gumbs

Heidi
John Gumbs

Just Mates

Sheila
John Gumbs

JAY G
Assignment to
The Netherlands
JOHN GUMBS

www.ingramcontent.com/pod-product-compliance
Lightning Source LLC
LaVergne TN
LVHW020313110826
845148LV00017BA/2652

9781787920101